Authors Of The Future

Edited By Debbie Killingworth

First published in Great Britain in 2023 by:

Young Writers
Remus House
Coltsfoot Drive
Peterborough
PE2 9BF
Telephone: 01733 890066
Website: www.youngwriters.co.uk

Printed and bound in the UK by BookPrintingUK
Website: www.bookprintinguk.com
YB0561I

Welcome!

Dear Reader,

Welcome to a world of imagination!

My First Story was designed for 5-7 year-olds as an introduction to creative writing and to promote an enjoyment of reading and writing from an early age.

The simple, fun storyboards give even the youngest and most reluctant writers the chance to become interested in literacy by giving them a framework within which to shape their ideas. Pupils could also choose to write without the storyboards, allowing older children to let their creativity flow as much as possible, encouraging the use of imagination and descriptive language.

We believe that seeing their work in print will inspire a love of reading and writing and give these young writers the confidence to develop their skills in the future.

There is nothing like the imagination of children, and this is reflected in the creativity and individuality of the stories in this anthology. I hope you'll enjoy reading their first stories as much as we have.

Imagine. .

Each child was given the beginning of a story and then chose one of five storyboards, using the pictures and their imagination to complete the tale. You can view the storyboards at the end of this book.

The Beginning...

One night Ellie was woken by a tapping at her window.

It was Robin the elf! "Would you like to go on an adventure?" he asked.

They flew above the rooftops. Soon they had arrived...

Contents

St Martin's CE (VA) Primary School, Fangfoss

Ella Taylor (6)	54
Isla Parker (7)	56
Jessica Hodgkinson (7)	57

St Peter's CE Primary School, Hindley

Olivia Robinson (7)	58
Callum Best (7)	60
Gracie Galvin (7)	62
Kylo Williams (6)	64
Nevaeh Jones (6)	65
Kenny Baxter (7)	66
Benjamin Park (6)	67
Isaac Weaver (6)	68
Indie Eatock (5)	69
Charlie Gee-Laithwaite (7)	70
Rose Hilton (7)	71
Harrison Spencer (7)	72
Heidi Eagle (7)	73
Cole Costello (7)	74
Elvis Jr Atem Tambe (6)	75
Theo Monaghan (6)	76
Scarlett Rose Beardsworth (6)	77
Tommy Taylor (6)	78
Isla Bleakley (5)	79
Sonny Fairhurst (6)	80
Emilia Blakeley (5)	81
Sophia Fouracre (6)	82
Grace May Roberts-Taylor (6)	83
Elsie Peers (5)	84
Niveen Saeed (6)	85

Starbank Primary School, Small Heath

Yumnah Chowdhury (6)	86
Sulaiman Muhammad (7)	87
Zeyneb Kchicech (6)	88
Faizah Jamil (7)	89

The Minster CE Primary School, Warminster

Willow Coath (7)	90
Freya Reid (7)	91
Poppy Watts (6)	92
Ava-Rivers Loveday (7)	93
Evie House (6)	94
Vivienne Carter (7)	95
Pippa Long (7)	96
Islay Chudley (7)	97
Drew Hadfield (7)	98
Jacob Mee (6)	99
Harry Kimber (6)	100

Whiteheath Infant & Nursery School, Ruislip

Hanna Becheroul (7)	101
Isla Hall (7)	102
Poppy Fisher (7)	104
Johnny Mulé (6)	106
Anaiya Grover (7)	108
Olivia Kretov (7)	110
Meriem Hadi (7)	112
Maisie Palmer (6)	113
Reya Idaikkadar (7)	114
Aranveer Dhanoa (7)	115
Eleanor Van Der Lee (7)	116
Archie Cooper (7)	117
Ella Morkunaite (7)	118
Edie Burton (6)	119
Innayah Mirza (7)	120
Lucas Liu (7)	121
Sara Paloja (7)	122
Amir-Saam Yazdizad (7)	123
Jack Hine (7)	124
Ruby Patel (7)	125
Manrai Sokhi (7)	126
Eliana Goodridge (6)	127
Esmé Mistry (7)	128
Kutay Baskurt (7)	129
Kaiyn Shah (7)	130
Connie Simmons (7)	131

The Stories

Ellie's Magical Adventure

Carefully, they clambered on a magical, enchanting unicorn and galloped off.
But suddenly a bloodthirsty, cold-hearted dragon appeared in front of them.
Suddenly the fire-breathing dragon was chasing the children and there were rushing feet, especially the teddy bear's.
Happily, the colourful, beautiful unicorn came back and the children jumped onto the beautiful unicorn and with a swish of her tail they galloped off into a new world.
But suddenly a wicked old witch appeared in front of them and cackled, then the terrifying children were very scared.
Luckily they stole the wicked witch's broom and they soared through the sky and the teddy bear was just dangling on the end.

Ellie Dack (7)
Cadland Primary School, Southampton

Zak's Magical Adventure

One dark night while everyone was asleep someone popped up at Ellie's glass window. It was Robin the elf. He said, "Hey, want to go on an adventure?"
Suddenly Roar, a colossal, bloodthirsty dragon, appeared out of nowhere. They ran for their lives until they found something...
But they still had to run from the colossal, bloodthirsty dragon but Robin had the perfect idea...
They took a lift on the beautiful, comfy unicorn and soared up the sky and went through the clouds until they found something mysterious but haunted.
It was a gloomy, cruel witch. She cackled because she suspected they couldn't escape. They felt nervous but they found something...

It was a spectacular broom. They went through the forest while the moon was bright and Ellie held on tight and in a few minutes they were home.

Zak Hackett (6)

Cadland Primary School, Southampton

3

Mollie's Magical Adventure

All of a sudden, Ellie and the elf came diving down onto a unicorn.

Suddenly they saw a huge scruffy dragon. They were petrified.

Quickly they ran to escape the green, terrifying, fiery dragon. Even the teddy named Brainy ran away.

Ellie and the elf hopped on the fluffy, colourful unicorn and soared into the sky. They felt happy because they had escaped the dragon.

Ellie and the elf saw a creepy witch. They were terrified. The witch said, "Eat this!" She was pointing at a lollipop so the teddy ate it. The teddy's eyes went all white in twenty seconds.

They rode on the witch's broomstick to their house. Ellie and the elf felt so happy they had got home.

Mollie Craggs (7)

Cadland Primary School, Southampton

4

Isabella's Magical Adventure

One night Ellie was in bed when suddenly she heard a knock on the door. It was Elf. He asked Ellie if she wanted to go on an adventure.

Next, they came to a gigantic, ferocious dragon. He appeared in front of them! The children started to quiver.

After that, the horrified children escaped the evil dragon by running as fast as they could to the colourful, beautiful unicorn.

Next, Elf and Ellie clambered onto the unicorn's back and galloped off to the forest.

Suddenly there was a crooked, creepy witch who appeared out of nowhere. She cackled but Elf managed to get her broom.

They got on the broom and flew off to their home.

Isabella Denham (7)

Cadland Primary School, Southampton

Jacob's Magical Adventure

Carefully Ellie clambered on the majestic, mythical unicorn.

Eventually, they landed. Suddenly a cold-hearted dragon appeared and Ellie and the elf were so surprised.

"Argh! The terrifying, cold-hearted dragon scared us off," said Ellie.

All of a sudden the dragon breathed scorching fire.

Afterwards, the beautiful, majestic unicorn appeared in a flash and went in a blink of an eye.

Suddenly a cackling laugh was heard and they swooped down. They saw an evil witch that cast a spell on them that gave them cleverness so the witch was cross.

They got the broom. They took off with Teddy hanging off the end.

Jacob Gaunt (7)
Cadland Primary School, Southampton

Dylan's Magical Adventure

All of a sudden, Ellie and Robin swooped down and landed on the floor of a pink and black cave.

Suddenly a colossal ruby dragon jumped out of the cave from behind her. Ellie was petrified.

The colossal ruby dragon was belching fireballs at Ellie and Teddy. The dragon scared the three children and they ran for their lives.

The unicorn soared and picked up Ellie, Robin and also Teddy and took them to a safe place. They felt delighted.

A creepy witch tried to trick them but the only one she tricked was Teddy.

They flew on the witch's broom and went straight home. They were relieved after their busy day.

Dylan Bicknell (6)

Cadland Primary School, Southampton

Imogen's Magical Adventure

One night, Ellie woke up and saw it was Robin the elf. He said, "Let's go on an adventure."

Ellie said, "Yes."

Suddenly, a colossal, fire-breathing dragon appeared. The children started to tremble. As soon as possible the children started running for their lives. They headed for the mythical, enchanted unicorn. They clambered onto their mythical, enchanted unicorn.

They soared through the sky and landed in a mythical land. They saw a cackling witch. She made their unicorn disappear.

The children stole the wicked witch's broom so they could get home.

Imogen Sandy (7)

Cadland Primary School, Southampton

Cody's Magical Adventure

Ellie and Robin clambered onto the mythical, magical unicorn.

After they flew they saw something so they decided to walk to it. It was a fire-breathing dragon.

They started to run because he was spitting fireballs at them and they were terrified.

Then they escaped the cold-hearted dragon with the cute teddy bear that Ellie brought, it was the only teddy she had.

They flew to a different place. The teddy was gifted a lollipop by a witch with a wrinkly face. They were terrified.

Finally, they quickly flew to Ellie's house at midnight. It was super dark so she went to sleep.

Cody Bridges (7)
Cadland Primary School, Southampton

Rogue's Magical Adventure

Jack and Ellie carefully clambered on a colourful, mythical unicorn.

Suddenly a terrifying, cold-hearted dragon ran up to them. Ellie and Jack were scared so they sprinted away.

Whilst they were running Ellie started to regret the adventure but something changed her mind...

It was the unicorn! The unicorn flew away to a strange place.

There was a witch. She said, "If you can beat me I'll give you my broomstick but you'll give me the unicorn." So they beat the witch.

Then they were flying home. When they arrived Ellie was exhausted so she went to bed.

Rogue Hawkins (7)

Cadland Primary School, Southampton

Eva's Magical Adventure

Ellie and Robin jumped on a unicorn one hot morning and they went on a magical adventure.

Next, they walked by a colossal, spiky dragon. The hideous dragon blew hot flames on Ellie and Robin. They were very scared.

Ellie, Robin and Teddy were being chased by the colossal dragon.

Ellie and Robin were saved by the unicorn and they were happy.

Ellie, Robin and Starfish were tricked by the witch who was putting sweets and lollies everywhere and the witch was getting them to drink her poison.

They escaped and they were so happy again. They went home.

Eva Morton (7)

Cadland Primary School, Southampton

Izzy's Magical Adventure

Robin the elf said, "Let's go on an adventure," so they hopped on a mythical, colourful unicorn and soared to a new world.

Suddenly a bloodthirsty, cold-hearted dragon attacked the kids.

So the children ran away from the dragon as fast as they could.

After that the children bumped into a beautiful, majestic unicorn and the children rode on it.

All of a sudden a creepy, wicked witch appeared out of nowhere. She gave the children a broomstick.

Finally, the children rode back home on the broomstick. It was an amazing adventure.

Izzy Phillips (7)

Cadland Primary School, Southampton

Ashley's Magical Adventure

One night Ellie was sleeping when she was woken up by Robin the elf. They clambered on a vibrant, unique unicorn.

All of a sudden, they soared into the air. They saw a bloodthirsty, evil dragon.

As quickly as they could they ran for their lives but then they were worried to see the dragon again.

After that, they galloped off on the majestic unicorn again and flew to another place.

Suddenly a cruel, evil witch appeared. She was trying to do an enchantment and she cackled.

Finally, they rode on the dark wooden broom and they went back home.

Ashley Wu (7)
Cadland Primary School, Southampton

Benjamin's Magical Adventure

One night, Robin the elf knocked at Ellie's door and then they clambered onto the mythical, colourful unicorn.

Suddenly a fierce, bloodthirsty dragon scared both of the children and then they ran off as fast as they could.

Then the dragon chased down the terrified children and it was not good. Then they nearly got set on fire.

Later they hopped back onto the unicorn and galloped off really fast.

Next, an ugly, wicked witch cackled at the children and they didn't like it.

Finally, they flew off on a broom and they went home.

Benjamin Sussex (7)

Cadland Primary School, Southampton

Skye's Magical Adventure

Once upon a time, there was a girl that was asleep. Her name was Ellie. Her friend Robin tapped on her window and they went on an adventure.

Suddenly a scary, colossal dragon appeared in front of Robin and Ellie and they ran away.

The kids ran away then the dragon breathed out fire, it was a scary dragon.

Then the unicorn appeared in front of Ellie and Robin the elf.

Later in the day, a creepy, gloomy witch came and she had an evil, cackling laugh.

Finally, Robin the elf took Ellie home on the witch's broomstick.

Skye Whitcher (7)

Cadland Primary School, Southampton

Sophia's Magical Adventure

First, the rainbow-sparkling unicorn galloped to the circus with a boy and a girl with a teddy bear.

Then, an evil, angry dragon breathed fire as it walked towards them.

Robin the elf and Ellie were running for their lives because the dragon was on their tails.

They ran and ran until they found the rainbow unicorn so they quickly clambered on her.

The dragon was gone so they went to get a lollipop. Suddenly a crooked witch was laughing at them.

The witch left but she forgot her broom so they flew home on it.

Sophia Thomas (7)

Cadland Primary School, Southampton

Lily-Lavigne's Magical Adventure

First, they went on a colourful, stonking unicorn. "This is so much fun!" said Ellie.
Then they saw a bloodthirsty, cold-blooded dragon and it nearly killed them with its sharp teeth.
The dragon was really mean so they quickly escaped.
Then they went back on the vibrant unicorn then jumped off the beautiful, vibrant unicorn.
Later they met a cruel witch. She cackled for two hours and it was so annoying.
Finally, the unicorn ran off so they stole the witch's broomstick and flew away up high.

Lily-Lavigne Farroll (7)

Cadland Primary School, Southampton

Edward's Magical Adventure

Once upon a time, there was a girl called Ellie. She heard a knock on the door and it was an elf called Robin.

Suddenly a colossal dragon appeared out of nowhere but they luckily escaped from it.

Next, they all ran away from the dragon with Teddy.

After that, they hopped back on the unicorn and went across the flat field.

Soon they saw some candy and a witch had it. She tried to give them poisonous candy but they attacked the witch and stole her broom.

They flew off home. They never saw the witch again.

Edward Hart (7)

Cadland Primary School, Southampton

Matthew's Magical Adventure

Suddenly Ellie and Robin dived quietly into the forest.

All of a sudden a bloodthirsty, ferocious dragon leapt out of a big tree. Ellie was petrified.

The ferocious dragon belched fire at Ellie and Robin. They rushed as quickly as a flash.

They hopped on the unicorn and flew above the clouds. They were ecstatic because they had escaped.

They eventually landed in front of a witch. She lured them into a trap.

But they defeated the witch and stole the witch's broomstick. They lived happily ever after.

Matthew Saintey (7)

Cadland Primary School, Southampton

19

Ciarán's Magical Adventure

All of a sudden Ellie with Robin swooped quietly on their unicorn.
Suddenly they landed in a cave of dragons then a bloodthirsty dragon appeared.
They ran away from the scaly, fire-breathing dragon. But in a flash, they escaped.
Next, they were fine, having a rest because they were scorching hot.
They got to a witch that was cruel and she tried to poison them but they stole her broom and flew off.
When it was night they flew home on the witch's broom. When they got home it was bedtime.

Ciarán Roberts (7)
Cadland Primary School, Southampton

Ellie's Magical Adventure

Carefully the children clambered on the magical rainbow unicorn's back.
Suddenly an evil, colossal dragon appeared. The dragon felt cold-hearted. Ellie and Robin were scared of the dragon.
Luckily the children were fast. They escaped the dragon.
They got back on the sparkling unicorn. They galloped to try to get home.
Suddenly a cruel wizard appeared. The wizard was old and evil.
Happily, Ellie and Robin flew off on a broomstick to their home.

Ellie Martin (7)

Cadland Primary School, Southampton

Charlie's Magical Adventure

One night when Ellie was asleep Robin horrendously banged on the window.
They clambered onto the unique unicorn then they accidentally rampaged into a fierce, horrid dragon.
Then the children sneakily escaped the cold-hearted dragon.
They jumped onto the unique, colourful unicorn's back and then flew off into thin air.
Later on, after the flight they met a cruel, crooked witch that cackled at them.
Finally, they flew home then said goodbye.

Charlie Howard (7)

Cadland Primary School, Southampton

Tyler's Magical Adventure

One night Ellie and Robin carefully got on the unicorn and rode off. They were excited.
Next, they met a bloodthirsty dragon and fire came out of his mouth.
Suddenly the bloodthirsty, evil dragon chased them. The dragon spat fire.
Later, they got on the beautiful, colourful unicorn and galloped away.
All of a sudden they met an old witch and she tried to trick them with candy.
Finally, Ellie and Robin got home on the witch's broomstick.

Tyler Manby (6)
Cadland Primary School, Southampton

Kaycee's Magical Adventure

Robin and Ellie hopped onto the pink unicorn.

Next, they saw an evil mean dragon. The dragon started to breathe burning fire.

Next, Ellie and Robin got chased by an evil humongous dragon.

After, Ellie and Robin escaped from the dragon. They got on the rainbow unicorn and flew away.

Later, Ellie and Robin met an evil witch. She tricked them with sweets.

Finally, Robin and Ellie took off with her broomstick and they went home.

Kaycee Price (6)

Cadland Primary School, Southampton

Max's Magical Adventure

The children clambered onto the enchanting, vibrant unicorn.

When they were galloping they came across a cold-hearted, bloodthirsty dragon.

The terrified children ran and Teddy ran away petrified.

So they got on the unicorn but Teddy had a paranoid feeling inside.

All of a sudden, a witch appeared in a puff of green, glowing smoke and tried to cast a spell on them.

Robin used his magic to steal her broom and fly home.

Max Dack (7)

Cadland Primary School, Southampton

George's Magical Adventure

One beautiful day Ellie and Robin went on a majestic adventure, riding on a unicorn.
Next, the evil dragon breathed fire at Ellie and Robin and they were very scared.
They hopped on their unicorn and they were scared and they ran away.
The wicked, old witch was creepy and after that they were scared and they ran away.
They hopped on the broom. They were nearly home with Teddy.
At last, they were finally home.

George Denham (7)

Cadland Primary School, Southampton

Esmai's Magical Adventure

Robin the elf clambered onto the colourful, mythical unicorn and they soared through the sky.

All of a sudden a ferocious dragon jumped out.

The kids were terrified. They ran away.

After that, Ellie came back and the kids hopped on and they soared through the sky.

Suddenly a creepy, wicked witch pointed at the kids and the kids were scared.

Finally, with a flash, they swooshed off and the kids went back home.

Esmai Critchlow (7)

Cadland Primary School, Southampton

Hugo's Magical Adventure

One night Ellie and Robin were riding a beautiful unicorn.

Later, they saw a fierce dragon and they were shocked. Ted hid behind Ellie.

Next, the fierce dragon chased them and ran away with Ted.

After that, they safely got onto the gold unicorn.

Suddenly, they came across an old witch. She tricked them with potions and sweeties.

Finally, they flew a yellow broomstick. Robin took Ellie home.

Hugo Abbott (6)

Cadland Primary School, Southampton

Kai's Magical Adventure

First, Ellie and Robin sat on a pink unicorn.
Next, a red dragon appeared. They were terrified.
The big dragon threw fire at them.
Next, they jumped onto the unicorn and flew away relieved.
A witch appeared and tried tricking them with her sweets.
Finally, they flew home on the witch's broomstick.

Kai Maidment (7)

Cadland Primary School, Southampton

Freddie's Magical Adventure

One sunny day Ellie and Robin went on a big adventure.
Suddenly an evil dragon blew fire at them. They were scared.
Ellie and Robin ran away from the dragon quickly.
After that, they were happy and safe.
On the way they saw a scary witch and they stole the witch's broom to fly back home.

Freddie Finch (6)

Cadland Primary School, Southampton

Amir's Jungle Adventure

Robin the elf and Ellie were swinging on the vine for fun with their teddy bear. They were swinging for a very long time until they landed.

They landed right next to a snake. They got terrified because it was a long one. It blended in with the colour green.

Robin the elf, Ellie and Teddy were running as fast as they could away from the snake and then they got no sight of the snake. They couldn't see a scale from the snake then they met a friendly lion called Leo.

Leo was so kind he let Robin the elf, Ellie and Teddy on his back. He ran, ran and ran until he got tired.

He dropped them at the edge of the jungle. They swung on the vines one more time then they reached home.

Amir Toutah (7)

Falconbrook Primary School, Battersea

Irem's Magical Adventure

Ellie and Robin the elf got on the unicorn and continued on their way.

Ellie and Robin the elf got scared by a dragon because they met the dragon on their way.

Ellie and Robin the elf were running away from the dragon towards the unicorn.

Ellie and Robin the elf got on the unicorn again and went on their way somewhere else.

Ellie and Robin the elf suddenly met a witch and they were very scared again but the witch was helping them.

The witch gave the flying broom to Ellie and Robin the elf. They returned home with the witch's flying broom and Ellie went back to bed.

Irem

Falconbrook Primary School, Battersea

Ebony's Zoo Adventure

...at the world's most magical zoo. And every animal was Robin's friend and they could talk.

Ellie said, "Where are we?" But then she saw the magical elephant and she knew.

The elephant said, "Go to the bamboo, you might see Panda."

At Bamboo Land, a giant panda was there with her baby. "Aww," said Ellie.

"We have got to go," said Robin.

As they went it got louder and louder. Ellie said, "What is that?"

Robin said it was Ollie the monkey.

Teddy liked climbing so he climbed the really tall tree. Ollie loved eating bananas so he shared one with Ellie.

Robin took Ellie home. "Goodbye," Robin said to Ellie.

"Goodbye," said Ellie.
So Robin walked off into the distance.

Ebony Oldham (7)
Matlock Bath Holy Trinity CE Controlled Primary
School, Matlock Bath

Oliver's Space Adventure

One night Ellie was woken by a tapping at the window. It was Robin the elf. "Would you like to go on an adventure?" he asked. They flew above the rooftops.

Soon they arrived on Jupiter. It was as cold as ice. Ellie made a rocket and spacesuit. Then she drove the rocket then suddenly a meteor hit the rocket then there was a big explosion. The rocket went into little pieces. Quickly Ellie caught all of the little bits of the rocket. Ellie looked up and saw Earth. It made the rocket turn back to normal. Ellie went in the rocket back home.

When Ellie was home she told everyone about space. People did not believe her so she proved it by showing videos and pictures. Then they believed her. Ellie's mum arranged a special party because Ellie was famous and they had games about space. They even invited people to the party. Ellie taught her friends about space.

Oliver Chew (6)

Sacred Heart RC Primary School, Colne

Annie-Lou's Space Story

There were two friends called Annie-Lou and Elsie.

One night Annie-Lou and Elsie were woken by a tapping at their window. It was Talula the elf. "Would you like to go on an adventure?" she asked.

They flew above the rooftops. Soon they arrived at Saturn, it was freezing cold. And on Saturn they saw a rocket flying. They asked the aliens, "Can we go in it?"

The aliens said, "Yay!" and they went in the rocket ship.

When they were in it they flew off and went to Jupiter. They went to all the rest of the planets. And then they went to the moon. Suddenly they crashed into a spaceship. The aliens said to the other aliens, "What have you done? You will pay for that! You fix it now!"

They said, "Let's just be friends."

"Okay, I am sorry."

"That's okay and I am sorry as well."

"That's okay."

Then they made up. Finally, they lived happily ever after.

Annie-Lou Braithwaite (6)

Sacred Heart RC Primary School, Colne

Louie's Space Adventure

One night, Elle was woken up by a tapping at her window. It was Robin the Elf!
"Would you like to go on an adventure?" he asked. They flew above the rooftops. Soon, they arrived at the end of the space. Elle is kind and is in space.
"No!" They forgot to turn. They crashed into Mars. They got out at Mars, they found a rock and a rope and saw aliens. The aliens were kind to Elle, they helped pull and they pulled the rocket out and them out and they arrived at Earth. They told all the people, no one believed her but her hand in her pocket pulled out a magic rock. They went home and got tired and put their toys away and their shirts away too, and they went to bed. They got up and got some food and put it in the rocket, and went home again and the door was locked. Elle knocked, but she realised she had the keys!

Louie Stock (6)

Sacred Heart RC Primary School, Colne

Talula's Space Adventure

One night, Ellie was woken by a tapping on her window. It was Robin the Elf!
"Would you like to go on an adventure?" he asked. They flew above the rooftops, they arrived at Mars. But Ellie needed to bring lots of summer clothes because it is the hottest place. Then they crashed. It was when they were getting off Mars and onto the rocket. Then she met some aliens and they thought that they might be good friends. So, the aliens took Ellie and the elf to where the aliens lived. Then they showed them around and they saw the houses that people had made, they made friends with the people who made houses and they helped them make their own house on the moon. They were shown around where they could work. Well, not everyone because they wouldn't be old enough for jobs and because there would not be enough room.

Talula Lonsdale (6)
Sacred Heart RC Primary School, Colne

Roksana's Space Adventure

One night Ellie was woken by a tapping at her window. It was Robin the elf. "Would you like to go on an adventure?" he asked. They flew above the rooftops. Soon they arrived at Jupiter. Ellie was hot, she felt like she was in a fire or a microwave! Then Ellie and Robin the elf made a spaceship and Ellie tried it out. "It works! It works!" Ellie screamed happily then she crashed into an alien's rocket ship.

Then they hopped out. She met the alien. His name was Billy Bob. Billy Bob was angry. They explained that they did not mean to. Billy Bob accepted Ellie's apology then Ellie fixed Billy Bob's rocket. He said thank you. Then Ellie and Robin the elf went into the rocket then they flew back to Earth. She went home and fell asleep in her bed.

Roksana Szerlag (6)
Sacred Heart RC Primary School, Colne

Florence's Space Adventure

One night Ellie was woken by a tapping at her window. It was Robin the elf. "Would you like to go on an adventure?" he asked. They flew above the rooftops. Soon they arrived... in space and landed on the moon. Then they just jumped and floated with the stars, the planets and also with each other. Ellie and Robin the elf saw a rocket the size of eight buses in a line. In the rocket there were nine aliens and the aliens were saying blee-blo blee-blo, which means hello and welcome. Ellie and Robin were floating up and down to get to the aliens. Suddenly they bumped heads on the rocket. They had a rock that was very cold for a cold compress. After feeling better they went home and kept it a secret and never told anybody only each other.

Florence Warriner (6)

Sacred Heart RC Primary School, Colne

Noah's Space Adventure

One night, Ellie was woken by a tapping at her window. It was Robin the Elf.

"Would you like to go on an adventure?" he asked. They flew above the rooftops.

Soon, they arrived. Now they were on the moon. But the moon was made of cheese! Next, they met an alien, a chef, and now they were eating. Next, the moon has been eaten! They fell into a meteor and now Ellie realised they had eaten all the moon and she told the others.

Robin said, "I can magic up one," and Ellie said yes, and Robin did his magic and now it is a rock moon. Now they just needed to go back to Earth. The alien said, "We can take you in a gobbledy-gook way and now they said, "Hop in," and they got in soon.

Noah Horsfield (6)

Sacred Heart RC Primary School, Colne

Betty's Space Adventure

One night Ellie was woken by a tapping at her window. It was Robin the elf. "Would you like to go on an adventure?" he asked. They flew above the rooftops. Soon they arrived at Saturn. Ellie met some aliens called George, Bash and Nelur.
They said. "Do you like music?"
"What is music?" said all the aliens.
When Ellie had heard the bad news she told Bash, George and Nelur. They were shocked by what they said. "You don't know what music is! You are insane!" they said all together at once.
Suddenly they heard tumbling, it was another rocket. It crashed. "You are insane as well! We have already had a crash!"

Betty Heap (6)
Sacred Heart RC Primary School, Colne

Molly's Space Adventure

One night Ellie was woken by a tapping at her window. It was Robin the elf. "Would you like to go on an adventure?" he asked. They flew above the rooftops. Soon they arrived on Jupiter. Then the rocket broke down so Ellie flew down to get some petrol. Ellie saved the day because she went to get some petrol. Ellie is a superstar and amazing.

When Ellie was in space she loved it. Then Robin the elf came up to her saying, "Are we going home?" As fast as she could she flew back to Jupiter to fill the rocket up with petrol. Then they played some games on Jupiter because they were so tired. Then they went home.

Molly Young (6)

Sacred Heart RC Primary School, Colne

Emilie's Space Adventure

One night, Ellie was woken by tapping at her window. It was Robin the Elf!
"Would you like to go on an adventure?" he asked. They flew above the rooftops. Soon, they arrived at Jupiter. Ellie was extremely cold! They saw aliens. Ellie wanted to visit the aliens. They were on their way, their spaceship broke down! The aliens were nice and they fixed the rocket! And the elf had special tools and he fixed it with them. When the elf fixed it, then they went back to Earth and Ellie told her mum, but her mum said, "No, I am in the middle of cooking." Then she listened.

Emilie Jeffries (5)
Sacred Heart RC Primary School, Colne

Emilia's Space Adventure

One night, Ellie was woken by a tapping at her window. It was Robin the Elf!
"Would you like to go on an adventure?" he asked. They flew above the rooftops. Soon, they arrived at Mars. On the way to Mars, they crashed into another rocket.
"Oh no!" they said. What would they do? Jim brought some tools in case they had a crash. They said, "Fyoofff." They fixed the rocket with the tools. It worked, then they said, "Hello, hello, how are you?" They made friends after they said hello. And they lived happily ever after.

Emilia Edwards (6)

Sacred Heart RC Primary School, Colne

Thomas' Space Story

One night Ellie was woken by a tapping on her window. It was Robin the elf. "Would you like to go on an adventure?" he asked. They flew above the rooftops. Soon they arrived in space. There was a rocket and glued on the rocket were lasers. Ellie and Robin got stuck onto the glue too! But luckily they got unstuck. Finally, they were safe. "Phew! That was close!"
They were finally safe. "Would you like to find a space rock?"
"Should we go home now?" asked Ellie.

Thomas Batley (6)
Sacred Heart RC Primary School, Colne

Reuben's Space Adventure

One night, Ellie was woken by a tapping at her window. It was Robin the Elf.
"Would you like to go on an adventure?" he asked. They flew above the rooftops, they arrived at the moon.
They met an alien on the moon, then they fell in a hole. Then they went on a shooting star. Then they fell off the shooting star, then they fell on their rocket. They went back to Earth, they told their friends.
They didn't believe her. Then she got her space rock, then they believed her.

Reuben Stacey (6)

Sacred Heart RC Primary School, Colne

Ella's Space Adventure

One night Ellie was woken by a tapping at her window. It was Robin the elf. "Would you like to go on an adventure?" he asked. They flew above the rooftops. They zoomed up to space. Soon they arrived on Mars. They crashed with some aliens. She said it was bad luck. They put the rocket back together, they magicked it.

Then they went back home with the rocket and she read a book at home. Soon her mum called teatime to Ellie and she had a hot dog.

Ella Jordan (6)

Sacred Heart RC Primary School, Colne

Race's Space Adventure

One night, Ellie was woken by a tapping at her window. It was Robin the Elf!
"Would you like to go on an adventure?" he asked. They flew above the rooftops. Soon, they arrived at Jupiter.
"Oh no! We have run out of fuel."
"But I have magic. We just need to wait a few seconds... There we go, our rocket is fine." Now we can go back home.
"Mummy, I have been to Jupiter! Look."
"Oh yeah!"

Race Kay (6)

Sacred Heart RC Primary School, Colne

Isaac's Space Adventure

One night Ellie was woken up by a tapping at her window. It was Robin the elf. "Would you like to go on an adventure?" he asked. They flew above the rooftops. Soon they arrived on Mars. They were in a rocket and they saw an alien in a rocket as well. They crashed into the aliens. Robin the elf was magic so he made two new rockets. One for the aliens and one for Ellie and Robin. Everybody was happy.

Isaac Whitehead (6)

Sacred Heart RC Primary School, Colne

Rosie's Space Adventure

One night, Ellie was woken by a tapping at her window. It was Robin the Elf!
"Would you like to go on an adventure?" he asked. They flew above the rooftops. Soon, they arrived at Saturn. It was extremely cold. Suddenly, aliens attacked their rocket, they blasted the door. Ellie and Robin went to Mars. They got out the window, then knocked the aliens off.
They went back to Earth.

Rosie Hill (6)

Sacred Heart RC Primary School, Colne

Talya's Space Adventure

One night Ellie was woken by tapping at her window. It was Robin the elf. "Would you like to go on an adventure?" he asked. They flew above the rooftops. Soon they arrived on a planet called Sweety Land. Sweety Land had lollipop trees with Haribos for leaves. Ellie flew into a marshmallow and got stuck! Suddenly a friendly alien came to help.
Soon she flew home.

Talya Barker (6)
Sacred Heart RC Primary School, Colne

Ella's Jungle Adventure

Soon they arrived on a magic island where plants and animals could talk. Ellie saw some vines hanging down from the sky.

"Can we go for a swing?" asked Ted.

They swung through the vines and fell on a tree branch and Ted landed on a snake's head. The snake was called Curly because he slept all curled up.

"Run away!" said Robin. "Curly looks very hungry!"

They ran deeper into the jungle. Strange-looking plants were whispering, "Find Leo, he will help you."

Ellie, Robin and Ted soon became lost in the dark jungle. *Roar! Roar!* A lion called Leo leapt out from behind the bushes.

"Please don't eat us," they cried.

"Don't worry, I can give you a ride home," Leo said. "Jump up on my back and I will take you back to the magic vines."

They happily swung back on the vines. "I'll drop you off back at your house," said Robin.

Ella Taylor (6)
St Martin's CE (VA) Primary School, Fangfoss

Isla's Jungle Adventure

...in a green leafy jungle. They used the strong vines to swing through the trees. They soon met a slithery green snake with red triangles on it. They had to get past him to carry on with their adventure.

Robin the elf had a plan. He would use his magic to make them run at lightning speed past the snake which they called Slitherun.

Next, a big golden lion jumped out from the trees and shocked Ellie and Robin.

They were quite surprised to see the lion was friendly and offered them a ride to the other side of the jungle. It was fast and bouncy.

Ellie could see her house in the distance so they grabbed the last vine and did a mighty big swing straight back into bed.

Isla Parker (7)

St Martin's CE (VA) Primary School, Fangfoss

Jessica's Jungle Adventure

...in the jungle. They swung through the trees on vines. It was fun.

They met a slithery snake called Simon. He was very funny and friendly.

Then Simon scared them. He wanted to eat Teddy so they ran away.

Then they saw a lion. It roared very loudly to say hello.

The lion gave them all a ride on his back.

They swung home on the vines. They had so much fun on their adventure.

Jessica Hodgkinson (7)

St Martin's CE (VA) Primary School, Fangfoss

Olivia's Magical Adventure

They went to Wonder Land and saw a beautiful princess and a unicorn. I saw that they were trapped in a witch's castle. They said, "Help us please!" Then we saw dancing sweets on an island, it was like a miracle. After that, we saw a naughty red dragon breathing out fire at us but luckily we got away from the scary dragon. Then we went back to the princess and unicorn to say goodbye to them. After a long walk looking for something else to do, we found a loveable witch at a candy home.

We thought the dancing sweets that we saw were following us to the candy house that the witch had. Then we decided to go in it, we thought we were going to be kidnapped. The witch put me in a cage and Ellie was trying to taste the witch's food. Luckily I got out of the cage and Ellie killed the witch so she could not get us. The next day I came to Ellie at 6 o'clock in the morning from Peter Pan and said, "Did you have a good time in Wonder Land?"

After that, we took off to Disneyland and we went into the magical car.

It took a very long time to get there but luckily we got there.

We went on lots of rides. We went to bed because we went in the middle of the day.

Then on day three, we said, "Shall we go on a couple of rides?"

"Let's go home."

"What shall we do at home now?"

"Let's go and play together with the mini car."

Olivia Robinson (7)
St Peter's CE Primary School, Hindley

Callum's Space Adventure

...at a brand new world where the stars were closer to the Earth. The girl was going with her teddy and Robin the elf. The boy told the girl that an alien was looking evil and laughing when they were collecting the stars. After they arrived they had five more stars left. The girl and the boy were pointing to the stars. "How many more do we need?" Aliens were sucking the girl and the teddy. The alien was controlling the girl to go inside the UFO. The teddy and the girl were floating. The girl was saying, "What's going on, how am I floating?"

The girl and the alien were waving at Robin the elf. They were going to the girl's home with her teddy inside the UFO. "I will see you Robin the elf when I'm home."

The alien, girl, Robin the elf and the teddy saw someone putting their tongue out. It was really mega long! They saw the frog with three eyes but in the UFO they said, "We have two eyes!"

Then, Robin, the girl, Teddy and also the alien waved goodbye. When the girl finally got home in the UFO they went to go inside their house.

Callum Best (7)

St Peter's CE Primary School, Hindley

Gracie's Amazing Adventure

Ellie and Robin arrived at Manchester. They heard a football match playing. A man approached them and he said, "Have you seen Ronaldo?"

Ellie said, "Who is he?"

The man said, "Oh I'm so sorry."

Then they went to the Manchester Carnival. They went on the stage. Nobody spotted them and they saw somebody singing. They danced for four hours.

After that, they got off stage and had a nap on Charlie's head. When they woke up they realised that it was 2am in the night. Robin said, "Oh no!"

Anyway, they went to Manchester Airport. They got a flight to Asia. They thought they were going to England and when they landed they were shocked! They ran, ran and ran.

Then they got their phones and booked the next flight to England. The flight was 10 hours long. They travelled and travelled until they got back. Hooray!

Gracie Galvin (7)
St Peter's CE Primary School, Hindley

Kylo's Jungle Adventure

First, they flew to the monkeys. The monkeys went 'oooaaah'. They had so much fun with the monkeys but they had to leave to go to the elephants.

When they got to the elephants they were so scared and terrified, they didn't have any fun, then they played with the babies.

Then they started to get chased by the elephants but the babies didn't. They were worried and scared but the mums and dads weren't. They wished they hadn't gone.

They went to the cheetahs. The cheetahs were scary but then they were friendly. They weren't excited but they had a lot of fun.

Then they had a piggyback. They had lots of fun. They were upset they had to leave before Ellie's mum knew where she was. Then they flew all the way to Ellie's house.

Kylo Williams (6)
St Peter's CE Primary School, Hindley

Nevaeh's Space Adventure

...in space. When Ellie and Robin arrived they put on their spacesuits and set off to see all of the planets. The moon and the sun were their favourites. They saw Earth, Mars, Venus and even Mercury.

Ellie said, "The galaxy was so cool! That really, really blew me away."

Robin the elf, said, "Are you having fun?"

"Yes!" said Ellie. "I am having the best time of my life!"

Robin said, "Ellie... Alligator!"

"Argh!" said both of them as the alligator came towards them.

They ran as fast as they could. Suddenly they heard a laughing sound. It turned out it was their friend, Mark.

"Mark!" they both said. They both ran to him. "Hooray!" they said.

Nevaeh Jones (6)

St Peter's CE Primary School, Hindley

Kenny's Jungle Adventure

Once, Robin the elf took Ellie to the jungle. They swung around the green vines and went from one to the other.

After that, they went to see a scary, green, slithering snake and the snake said, "I'm very, very tired."

But he lied and then he said, "I'm going to get you!"

Ellie, Robin and the bear ran away and they said, "Phew!"

Next, they got lost and a friendly lion popped up in the bushes. He said, "Do you want a ride on my back?"

They said, "Yes."

While they were riding on his back the lion said, "Where do you live?"

"Next to a brown and green tree."

"Okay."

Finally, they swung and swung till they got home.

Kenny Baxter (7)
St Peter's CE Primary School, Hindley

66

Benjamin's Zoo Adventure

They went to the zoo and Robin said, "Let's look at the animals."

"We might see lots of animals," said Ellie.

They said they would have fun.

They went to an animal right away. They went on an elephant. It was a long journey but it was worth it.

Then they went on a panda ride. Then when they got off they had a cuddle with a panda and they saw a baby panda.

They went on the elephant again. They went a different way. They went through lots of trees.

They fell off and they ate like gorillas. Now they wanted to swing! They didn't know why the gorilla was standing up.

Robin went to Ellie's home. Then Robin went home on the elephant. They said goodbye to each other.

Benjamin Park (6)

St Peter's CE Primary School, Hindley

Isaac's Zoo Adventure

One night Ellie got woken up by a boy called Robin the elf. They went to the zoo which had loads of animals.

When they got there they rode an elephant with Ellie's teddy bear on the trunk. They really liked playing on the elephant.

After that Robin the elf flew to a panda and Ellie went too. Ellie cuddled the panda and the panda cuddled her back. The panda had two babies.

They went back on the elephant with the teddy bear tangled in the trunk. They were going back home.

On the way back they saw a monkey. He was nice and fluffy. He wanted to share his banana with her.

Then she went back home because it was night-time. They both said bye and she took her teddy bear.

Isaac Weaver (6)

St Peter's CE Primary School, Hindley

Indie's First Story

The old lady was watering the plants. There was a unicorn lying down on the grass. The lady who owned the garden looked after the unicorn.

Then there was an old man who came out with some children. He said, "Can the children play in the back garden with the unicorn?"

The lady said, "Of course they can."

The children played in the garden and the lady asked if they would like to ride the unicorn.

They lined up one by one and went on the unicorn for a ride. They had the best time playing in the garden.

The children said thank you to the lady for letting them ride the unicorn. They lived happily ever after.

Indie Eatock (5)

St Peter's CE Primary School, Hindley

Charlie's Savannah Adventure

Suddenly, a cheetah approached with a jump scare at the savannah at the girl. Then she fell over on the hard floor which was very dirty.

After that, a very suspicious lion was behind Robin the elf. It was going to attack him, it thought he was prey.

Then a hippo came along, just walking past them. Later a rhino was chasing Robin and the girl.

Then they saw a giraffe eating leaves on a tree. There was only one leaf left so they found some more.

Suddenly the giraffe was thankful so the giraffe gave them some chocolate, yum! Do you love chocolate?

Finally, when they were going to go home they saw a tiger and a black hippo.

Charlie Gee-Laithwaite (7)

St Peter's CE Primary School, Hindley

Rose's Amazing Adventure

In Magic Land the king is Stitch and the queen is Angel. Then they came down and walked to the palace.

When they got to the palace they saw King Stitch and the king came to Ellie.

He said, "We are being attacked."

Then the queen came in and said, "You are the only one that can help us, please help."

Then the maid came in to say, "They're coming this way!"

So they went to attack. An hour later they finally won.

Then they went outside and everyone said, "Ellie, Ellie!"

The king and queen said, "Do you want to stay?"

"Yes please."

Rose Hilton (7)

St Peter's CE Primary School, Hindley

Harrison's Zoo Adventure

The elf took the girl to the zoo and they saw an elephant but they ignored it and went in. As soon as they could they had a ride on an elephant and a little teddy went on it as well. The girl had popcorn and cold Coke. The elephant took them to a panda and the elf was holding a baby panda and the girl hugged him.

Then the elephant took them to a monkey called Banana. He was eating a banana, and the girl was.

They were smiling because the banana was good and then the teddy was swinging in the trees, he wanted to be a monkey.

Then the elf was smiling and saying goodbye and the girl was waving to the elf.

Harrison Spencer (7)

St Peter's CE Primary School, Hindley

Heidi's Zoo Adventure

...at the zoo. When they approached there was a dark grey, cheeky and a most mischievous looking elephant trying to escape the zoo.

When the elephant escaped the zoo the crazy elf and Ellie and her teddy jumped on and travelled to the panda.

When they arrived, Ellie and her teddy hugged the panda and Robin was too interested in his new panda teddy.

After that, the elephant took his three special friends to see the monkeys.

They arrived at the monkeys but only Ellie and her teddy were there because Robin didn't like monkeys.

Finally, the dark grey elephant took Ellie and her teddy home.

Heidi Eagle (7)

St Peter's CE Primary School, Hindley

Cole's Jungle Adventure

One day there was an elf called Robin and he was going on an adventure through the jungle.

Then Robin saw a snake and the snake almost ate him but he got away.

Robin was running through the jungle and then he saw some bushes and saw a lion. Then Robin rode on the lion and came off it and saw a crocodile and shouted.

It went into the water. Then he saw cheetahs running really, really fast. After that he saw a cow eating grass and Robin took some milk out of it. Then he saw some pigs.

Cole Costello (7)

St Peter's CE Primary School, Hindley

Elvis' Amazing Adventure

In this story... Max could run so fast.

One day they were in the woods when they saw a big 'K' in the middle of nowhere. It was blue and shiny. They had started to worry about it when Max got pulled by... nothing.

He cried for help. No one heard him but he ran his fastest and it worked. He ran for his life.

He noticed he was getting pulled into a hole then he fell in. He ran out like I said and he never went to the woods again. Why do you think Max ran? Then his hair turned blue!

Elvis Jr Atem Tambe (6)

St Peter's CE Primary School, Hindley

Theo's Space Adventure

We flew to space looking at the stars and planets. We flew higher and higher. When we got to the moon I started to collect stars but little did we know an alien was spying on us.

We got abducted and Ellie was scared but I knew he was good because we were friends. I told Ellie he was nice and then she felt better. We explored planets.

When we reached our first planet there was a bad alien with three eyes, eight legs and two arms.

We finally dropped Ellie off at her home.

Theo Monaghan (6)

St Peter's CE Primary School, Hindley

Scarlett's Space Adventure

One night Ellie was woken by a tapping at her window. It was Robin the elf. "Would you like to go on an adventure?" he asked. They flew above the rooftops.

As soon as they arrived at the moon they were touching the stars. Then they met an alien but then the alien sucked them into his spaceship.

They flew in the alien's spaceship.

But suddenly when they were about to land there was a big monster.

But finally, they dropped Ellie back at her house.

Scarlett Rose Beardsworth (6)

St Peter's CE Primary School, Hindley

Tommy's Space Adventure

One night, Ellie heard a noise. It was Robin the elf. They went on an adventure together.

They flew high over the rooftops and mountains and they landed in space.

They saw the world from the moon and they met some friendly aliens.

They were all enjoying a yummy picnic when suddenly Robin got sucked up into a black hole.

Ellie found some special powder in her pocket which helped Robin into the aeroplane so that he could get out of the black hole.

Tommy Taylor (6)

St Peter's CE Primary School, Hindley

Isla's Space Adventure

One night Ellie was asleep when Robin the elf knocked on Ellie's window.
Ellie and Robin the elf flew to the moon.
And then together they went on the moon.
Next, the alien got them in his trap. They got trapped at the top of the moon.
Then Ellie was happy and even the alien was too. Then they went into the alien's ship.

Isla Bleakley (5)

St Peter's CE Primary School, Hindley

Sonny's Space Adventure

One night Ellie got woken up by an elf called Robin. He wanted to see Mars and he was shouting, "Neil Armstrong!" at her. He was waving his hand.

The elf and the girl got sucked up by an alien invasion and they never got found. The alien kept laughing because he'd got the girl and the elf.

Sonny Fairhurst (6)

St Peter's CE Primary School, Hindley

Emilia's Amazing Adventure

The flamingos were playing and they were relaxed.

Two little bunnies were hopping along. Hop hop hop...

And one more bunny came along and they all jumped up and said, "Bunny power makes the dream work!"

And one more bunny came hopping along.

Then they saw a beautiful tree.

Emilia Blakeley (5)

St Peter's CE Primary School, Hindley

Sophia's Magical Adventure

They found a unicorn and they wanted to ride it.

And then they met a dragon who roared at them.

And then they ran away.

They got back on the unicorn and rode on it.

And then they met a witch.

They got a broomstick and got away.

Sophia Fouracre (6)

St Peter's CE Primary School, Hindley

Grace's Space Adventure

The children were happy.

The alien was staring.

The alien sucked up the children.

They were happy.

Fear was a monster.

Then they took the little girl back home.

Grace May Roberts-Taylor (6)

St Peter's CE Primary School, Hindley

Elsie's Magical Adventure

They were riding a unicorn.
The dragon was scaring the children.
The dragon was breathing fire.
The unicorn could fly.
The witch was evil.
They flew back home.

Elsie Peers (5)

St Peter's CE Primary School, Hindley

Niveen's Zoo Adventure

She went to the zoo.
The zoo was fun.
She had a lot of fun.
The bear had lots of fun.
She ate a banana.
She said bye.

Niveen Saeed (6)
St Peter's CE Primary School, Hindley

Yumnah's Magical Adventure

...at a beautiful, big, green field. Ellie and Robin had lots of fun playing under the tall tree.

Suddenly, a fierce red dragon blew flames at Ellie and Robin. "Run Ellie, run!" said Robin.

Ellie, Robin and Teddy ran as fast as they could from the evil dragon. Soon, they managed to escape from the dragon.

When they were free from the dragon, Robin said, "Let's explore this magical hill." Ellie agreed.

After some time, an old, nasty and grumpy witch approached Robin and Ellie. "Would you like some sweet candy?" asked the old witch.

Robin, Ellie and Teddy pushed the old witch down the hill, got onto her broomstick and finally flew back home to safety.

Yumnah Chowdhury (6)
Starbank Primary School, Small Heath

Sulaiman's Jungle Adventure

First, they were swinging on the soft, brown tree branches.

They arrived at the jungle but then they were shocked because there was a green, slithery snake in front of them.

The horrible snake chased after the scared children and they were trying to get away from the snake.

After that, a fearless lion came and scared the terrible snake away and the children were happy.

Next, the children hopped on the lion's back and went home.

Finally, when they got home they lived happily ever after.

Sulaiman Muhammad (7)

Starbank Primary School, Small Heath

Zeyneb's Pirate Adventure

Once upon a time, there was a little girl called Ellie. One day she woke up and went out. She saw her friend and they went on a pirate adventure.

Ellie and her friend, Robin, found a treasure chest with gold in it but there was a pirate chasing them.

The pirate was shouting at them and he was mean and nasty. He then took the chest with him. He made Ellie and Robin fall off the boat.

They jumped on a dolphin and then arrived home happily ever after.

Zeyneb Kchicech (6)

Starbank Primary School, Small Heath

Faizah's Zoo Adventure

One day a little girl and a little boy wanted to go to the zoo so they went to the zoo. They went to see an elephant and the elephant let the two children on its back. They then went to see a panda and they even found out the panda had a baby panda.

They then went to find a new animal and they found a monkey. The monkey was so nice he gave the little girl a banana.

They then had to say goodbye.

Faizah Jamil (7)

Starbank Primary School, Small Heath

Willow's Magical Adventure

...on a magical unicorn. It was beautiful, sparkly and colourful. Robin and Ellie loved it. It was so amazing. Soon Ellie felt scared of how high she was.

After that, they heard a rumbling. The unicorn was scared so she ran away. The noise got closer and closer. "A dragon!" they both shouted. It was breathing fire! They landed as quickly as they could. "It is so hard to run with little legs," Ellie said. "It's hard to run with elf legs," said Robin.

Soon they caught a ride on a unicorn. The sun was shining and there was a beautiful blue sky. Ellie loved it.

Then they saw some candy canes and some delicious gummy bears near a house where the old lady stood.

Then the old lady tried to lure them in but whilst she was making a potion, they took her broomstick and flew out of the door all the way home.

Willow Coath (7)

The Minster CE Primary School, Warminster

Freya's Jungle Adventure

...at a sweltering jungle. There was only a tiny bit of space but luckily Ellie had an idea. "Swing on the vines," said Ellie.

But when they landed on a tree there was a slithering snake. Ellie had an idea.

"Remember the vines?" said Ellie. "We could climb down them."

But that didn't work. "The only idea left is to run!" shouted Ellie. Finally, they got away from the snake so they jumped down from the tree.

Standing next to them was a lion but it wasn't a mean, vicious lion, it was a kind, friendly lion.

The lion roared. *It probably meant hop on,* thought Ellie. So did Robin. So they did. The lion pounced around the jungle.

In the end, they came back home so they swung on the vines and said bye to the lion. Ellie walked up the path and said bye to Robin and went into the house.

Freya Reid (7)

The Minster CE Primary School, Warminster

Poppy's Magical Adventure

...on a unicorn, a pink fluffy unicorn. They travelled high and low in the sun. Ellie said, "Wow, what's this place?"

"It's Fairy Land," said Robin.

Next, Ellie and Robin saw a dragon, it was terrifying. It was breathing out fire. "Argh!" said Ellie.

"Run!" said Robin. They ran so fast.

When Ellie and Robin were running from the dragon it was still breathing fire and flapping its wings.

When they were running they saw the unicorn so they hopped on. "Go, go, go!" said Ellie but the unicorn dropped Ellie and Robin at a wicked witch.

"Oh no," said Robin, "not the wicked witch. Run."

"Get on the broomstick," said Ellie, so they did. Suddenly, Ellie was in her bed and she fell asleep.

Poppy Watts (6)

The Minster CE Primary School, Warminster

Ava-Rivers' Magical Adventure

...at a magical wood. It was really big and it had lots of trees and grass. She saw the big sun, rivers and a path. They then saw a real unicorn.

They heard a noise and it frightened the unicorn. It was a bad dragon so they ran away. It came closer and closer.

When Robin and Ellie ran away they ran to the mountains but the dragon was still chasing them. They then saw something in the distance behind a tree. It was the unicorn so they quickly ran to it. The unicorn ran and then flew.

They landed next to a witch with a sweetie house the witch was living in. As the witch said hello in a creepy voice they ran away. It was nearly the morning so they went really fast. They got the witch's broomstick and then sneaked away and arrived home.

Ava-Rivers Loveday (7)

The Minster CE Primary School, Warminster

Evie's Magical Adventure

...they landed in a magical place and they saw a unicorn. They jumped onto the unicorn. When they were riding they saw a dragon.

They were frightened. They stood together. The dragon blew some fire at them and the dragon was mad. They then got a plan.

Their plan was to run. They ran and ran as fast as they could. The dragon was blowing fire with his mighty roar.

They saw the unicorn, jumped onto it and quickly rode off. They said, "Thank you."

Then they saw a wicked witch. The witch was evil and said, "I would eat you all up but I already have Hansel and Gretel. I will eat you next time."

Then the witch gave them a broomstick and they whooshed off. They slowed down because they were back home.

Evie House (6)

The Minster CE Primary School, Warminster

Vivienne's Forest Adventure

...at a deep, old and dark forest in Scotland. Ellie tapped Robin on the shoulder and pointed to a crow's nest. It was a horrible sight to see.

Suddenly, Ellie walked into some sticky mud so she shouted. Robin went to get some help.

Suddenly, she got picked up by a bird unicorn and it told Ellie her name was Pearl and she wanted to be friends.

"Yes! Of course," said Ellie. "Why didn't you say so?"

"I was afraid you would say no."

"Why would you think that?"

"I don't know," said Pearl.

"Good," said Robin.

"Look!" said Emily. "A bat dragon!"

"Oh no!" said Robin and Ellie together.

Vivienne Carter (7)
The Minster CE Primary School, Warminster

Pippa's Magical Adventure

...at a magical forest. Very soon they saw a unicorn. The unicorn was nice. She flew them to her home and then they went somewhere else. The unicorn couldn't find them.

They saw a dragon, a fire-breathing dragon. Soon the unicorn appeared and they ran to the unicorn. They were saved. The unicorn disappeared. "Where are you going?" the elf said.

The sun was going down and the full moon was rising. A witch came out. She said, "Hello, I am lonely. Can you please stay with me?"

"No," said the elf.

The witch said, "I'll put you in my pot."

They stole her broomstick and flew off to their home and said, "I want to do that again!"

Pippa Long (7)

The Minster CE Primary School, Warminster

Islay's Winter Wonderland Adventure

They landed in a house. In the house, there was a girl called Lucy. She was playing hide-and-seek. There was a wardrobe so Lucy went to hide in there.

Robin said, "Can we come too?"

"Yes," said Lucy.

In they went and when they went in there was snow. It was a winter wonderland but they did not know there was a waterfall coming up. Lucy kept on walking and she didn't see the waterfall and she fell into it. They dived down the cliff. When they got to the bottom they dived in and found Lucy. When they got out the snow was melting so it was almost spring.

After a while, it was time to go home so they set off.

Islay Chudley (7)

The Minster CE Primary School, Warminster

97

Drew's Space Adventure

...at Mars! It was red, dusty with lots of craters and it was strange! They were shocked because they thought they were going somewhere else.

They found a nearby planet and jumped to it because they both saw aliens coming to them on Mars! Two jumped onto the other planet.

Ellie and Robin were sucked up by a UFO! The two aliens and the UFO were camouflaged making them impossible to see.

Ellie and Robin opened a door to see a deploy pod with two seats. They sprinted to the deploy pod seats but the aliens followed but they were too slow and sloth-like.

In a flash of light, Ellie and Robin found themselves back at home.

Drew Hadfield (7)

The Minster CE Primary School, Warminster

Jacob's Jungle Adventure

They swung through the green vines. Soon they arrived at a sweltering hotel.
They left in about ten minutes. They bumped into a snake, it was poisonous.
"Run, it's going to eat us." Soon they lost it.
"I hope it's gone," said the teddy bear.
Suddenly, a lion pounced out of the bushes. They stopped for a minute and he was scared.
He started to get used to them quite quickly and they became friends. They went on a quiet ride.
They swung off back to their home through the vines and went to bed. "Goodnight."

Jacob Mee (6)
The Minster CE Primary School, Warminster

Harry's Jungle Adventure

...and they landed in a familiar jungle so they swung through branches and then stopped. They heard a hiss.

A snake appeared. It had a pattern on the back of it. It hissed at Ellie.

The snake chased them along the tree trunk. The slimy snake stopped and stood tall.

After they ran into a lion. The lion growled at them but he was friendly.

They rode the lion and he was quite fast. He ran as fast as he could.

They swung in the branches at night and swung to their house. The bear held on tight.

Harry Kimber (6)

The Minster CE Primary School, Warminster

Hanna's Jungle Adventure

Ellie and the elf went on an adventure to the jungle. They met some kind monkeys. Ellie and the elf decided to swing with the happy monkeys and stayed for a camp.

The next day they met a colourful, shiny snake. They thought the snake was evil but the snake was not evil so Ellie and the elf stayed for a camp again.

At night they heard the snake was evil. The snake was pretending to be a good snake so they ran away.

Ellie and the elf were walking along and suddenly they met a fierce, scary lion but it wasn't scary or fierce after all.

The lion took Ellie and the elf on a ride. It was a long, fast ride. Ellie and the elf really enjoyed the ride.

The lion took Ellie and the elf to some vines. Ellie and the elf swung on the vines then Ellie saw her house and went in and said bye to the elf.

Hanna Becheroul (7)

Whiteheath Infant & Nursery School, Ruislip

Isla's Zoo Adventure

Suddenly Ellie, Teddy and Robin the elf arrived outside the zoo gates. Ellie was surprised, she saw a very tall, spotty giraffe peeking over the yellow zoo gates, and a grey, wrinkly elephant.

Five minutes later Nessy the elephant gave Ellie, Teddy and Robin a ride on her grey, wrinkly back. They saw lots of beautiful sights.

Then Ellie, Teddy and Robin the elf came to a stop and met Pandy the white and black panda. Ellie hugged Pandy and Pandy hugged Teddy. Robin hugged one of Pandy's panda babies.

After, when they got back on Nessy's wrinkly grey back Robin spotted another sight, of monkeys and gorillas eating bananas. Ellie loved bananas.

They joined the monkeys and gorillas. Ellie ate bananas with the monkeys and gorillas while Teddy swung on a long green vine. Ellie loved eating bananas with the monkeys and gorillas.

After, they went out of the zoo gates and back home. Ellie was sad to leave the zoo and say goodbye to all her friends but she knew to go there next time.

Isla Hall (7)
Whiteheath Infant & Nursery School, Ruislip

Poppy's Zoo Adventure

"We're at the zoo!" said Ellie yawning. "And I can already see an elephant's trunk around the sign that says 'zoo'!"

"Come on, what are you waiting for? We haven't even had one of the fun parts yet," so they got on an elephant's back and asked for a tour.

He said, "Yes!"

They went to Mother Panda who had some babies. They held one of the babies and had a great time, they were very soft!

After that, they hopped on the elephant's back again. "Where are we going to go next?" said Ellie.

"You'll see," said Robin.

"We're at the monkeys!" she said. "And look at that big one over there!" It was a daddy monkey. They went to go chat to him and have a banana.

Then Ellie said, "I am a bit tired."
Robin took her home and said, "Goodnight Ellie."
She said back to him, "Goodnight."

Poppy Fisher (7)

Whiteheath Infant & Nursery School, Ruislip

Johnny's Zoo Adventure

...at the zoo. Then they climbed onto a grey, wrinkly elephant and stomped all around the zoo.

He took them to the panda area where they met a fluffy baby panda and its mummy.

They stayed for a little while but then had to go, there were more animals to see.

Ellie and Robin searched the zoo for Ellie's favourite animal, the chimpanzee!

"Where are they?" she asked quietly.

"Tada!" said Robin the elf excitedly.

Ellie sat down with Charlie the chimp and ate a sweet, tasty banana, while her snuggly bear, Ted, swung on some vines.

Then Robin said, "It's time to go."

Ellie was sad to leave the zoo, but she'd had a wonderful time with Robin and the animals and she was ready to go back home.

"Bye," said Ellie.

"Until next time!" giggled Robin the elf as he vanished into thin air.

Johnny Mulé (6)

Whiteheath Infant & Nursery School, Ruislip

Anaiya's Jungle Adventure

They arrived at a green, red, orange, yellow, blue, purple, pink, brown, black rainforest. In the sky there was a colourful rainbow. There were hundreds of green trees.

On the journey through the jungle they met a green scaly snake who slithered forward to Ellie and Robin the elf.

The snake said, "I will eat you up!"

"Argh!" said Ellie and Robin the elf. They started running. Soon their feet got tired so they stopped.

When they stopped they met a nice, big lion. The lion said, "Are you lost?"

Ellie and Robin the elf said, "Yes, we are looking for food."

They hopped to a fruit patch. It took them ten minutes to get there. In the meantime, they listened to the sounds. They finally arrived after a long ride.

They picked some delicious fruits then Robin the elf took Ellie back home to see her parents.

Anaiya Grover (7)

Whiteheath Infant & Nursery School, Ruislip

Olivia's Jungle Adventure

...in the jungle. Robin swung on the vines and met a cute, cuddly bear. "Come, Ellie," Robin said and they both swung on the vines, *whoosh!*

Then they met a green and friendly snake but Robin and Ellie were scared so the snake tried to prove that he was friendly. He moved so they could go but he was joking, he was a nasty snake and he chased them through the jungle.

The snake gave up on chasing them so they were safe. Phew!

Then they met a lion. He told Ellie and Robin that he was actually friendly. "Yay!" said Ellie.

Next, Ellie said, "Can we ride on you?"

"Yes, you may."

So they rode on the lion with the bear and then they swung on the vines while saying goodbye. "Bye-bye."
Ellie saw her home so she went.

Olivia Kretov (7)

Whiteheath Infant & Nursery School, Ruislip

Meriem's Jungle Adventure

They went on the green, smooth vines. Swinging along the jungle, going right and left, going backwards and forwards.

They had to get off the vines. "We can't be on the vines forever!" So they were walking along the path and they saw a snake so they ran. Teddy tried so hard to catch up and he did. They were running and running to get away from the snake.

So they got away from the snake. Then they bumped into the lion. The lion was very friendly so they talked to him a little.

He allowed them to ride on him back to their home and they arrived back at the vines.

"Bye," said the lion. They said, "Bye," too then they hopped onto the vines. They swung and then they went home. "Bye," they said to each other.

Meriem Hadi (7)

Whiteheath Infant & Nursery School, Ruislip

Maisie's Jungle Adventure

Ellie and Robin were flying on top of the rooftops and they saw a portal. They went through it and suddenly they were swinging on the jungle vines in the green land. Ellie said, "This is fun!" But they had to stop because there were no more vines.

They walked a little bit and saw a snake. They said, "Argh!" and ran away.

They ran and ran as fast as they could. The snake was following them too. They said, "Argh!" again.

They met a lion and he was purring up behind the leaves. He had a big yellow mane and he seemed friendly, and he was! They jumped on the lion's back and the lion leapt into the green lands.

They jumped back on the vines and they swung vine to vine and finally, they got back home.

Maisie Palmer (6)

Whiteheath Infant & Nursery School, Ruislip

Reya's Zoo Adventure

Suddenly Ellie felt like she had landed. She opened her glimmering green eyes and saw she was at the zoo. There was a tall, spotty giraffe peeking over the fence.

Soon they saw a dry, wrinkly elephant and it gave them a bumpy ride all the way to the warm, cuddly pandas.

They saw one eating long, yummy bamboo. Robin the elf even got to cuddle a baby panda!

They hopped back on the grey, slow elephant for another ride. It was very fun. Next, they found that they were in the monkey area. One of them gave Ellie a banana. It was tasty! Ellie's teddy played on some long, green vines.

After, it was time to go. Ellie was disappointed to leave but she had had a great time with Robin the elf and the animals at the zoo.

Reya Idaikkadar (7)

Whiteheath Infant & Nursery School, Ruislip

Aranveer's Jungle Adventure

Ellie and Robin the elf flew above the rooftops to a dark, creepy, scary jungle. Swinging across the vines they reached the trees that the king snake lived in.

Shocked, they froze, frightened. The king snake hissed as loud as his hissing tongue could.

They ran since they didn't know what to do. For some reason, the snake wasn't chasing them but then they saw a lion.

They were very confused because usually a lion attacks people but they realised the lion was a friendly lion.

So they rode off on the male adult lion's back. They trusted the only friendly lion. The lion said his name was Max. "Hi Max!"

Ellie, Robin the elf and Ellie's teddy thanked Max and swung back home.

Aranveer Dhanoa (7)

Whiteheath Infant & Nursery School, Ruislip

Eleanor's Jungle Adventure

...at the dark green jungle in the middle of nowhere.

It was as black as the road and they swung on deep green vines.

Then they met Kaa, the creepy snake. Ellie was scared. Kaa tried to trick Ellie. Ellie did not speak.

They both noticed Kaa tricked them so they ran away to protect themselves.

Then they met Mufasa, the king of the jungle. At first, Ellie was scared and then they became best friends.

Before Ellie could even blink, they were on the lion's back, strolling across the jungle. The lion tossed them on the green vines above them. They swung to Ellie's house. She climbed into her window and fell asleep in her bed.

Eleanor Van Der Lee (7)

Whiteheath Infant & Nursery School, Ruislip

Archie's Jungle Adventure

...in the mighty jungle. They found a cute brown bear. The bear wanted to play so they swung on some vines until they met Sid the scary snake. He hissed at Ellie, Robin the elf and Bear. They were frightened.

They ran scaredly and fast. They were running and running until Sid the snake didn't see them. They were safe.

Then they met a friendly lion called Thomas. Ellie, Robin and Bear were confused because Thomas the tiger was vegan.

And he didn't want to eat them. He wanted to take them home safely. They were having lots of fun.

They were going back home safely to go back to sleep. They were jumping back home for a good sleep.

Archie Cooper (7)

Whiteheath Infant & Nursery School, Ruislip

Ella's Jungle Adventure

...in the jungle. There was a tall tree. They climbed it and Ellie saw the whole jungle. They swung off the tree and met a snake. It looked fierce and scary. Ellie was frightened. Then the snake wanted to get them.

They ran as fast as their legs could go but just in time... *Bang!*

A lion saved them. It was a kind one with a big mane and sharp claws. He said, "Do you want a ride home?"

"Yes please," Ellie said.

"Let's go!"

They went on a shortcut towards their home.

When they were near their home the lion left and they continued on the jungle's swinging vines.

Ella Morkunaite (7)

Whiteheath Infant & Nursery School, Ruislip

Edie's Jungle Adventure

They swung from vine to vine to reach the jungle. A little brown teddy bear followed behind them and it was very fun. "Whooo!" said the teddy bear.

But a snake slithered in front of them and they couldn't go in front of the snake but then they created a distraction by saying, "Bye, I am going to go!" and they ran off. Then they saw a friendly lion. They looked scared but the lion was very happy then the lion swung them onto his back and the little brown teddy bear was on the lion's head. They swung vine to vine all the way home. Ellie, Robin and the teddy bear were feeling very happy.

Edie Burton (6)
Whiteheath Infant & Nursery School, Ruislip

Innayah's Zoo Adventure

...at the zoo, but the animals were not in cages. Once they got in there they went on an elephant. Ellie was so excited.

Robin the elf took Ellie to the elephant. She loved it. She climbed on the elephant and rode it. She loved it so much.

Ellie went to see the pandas. She hugged them. Robin hugged a baby panda. They loved it so much.

After that Ellie went on the elephant. She loved it so much. She shouted, "Yay!" She loved it.

She went to see the monkey. Ellie sat down and ate a banana.

Then Robin dropped Ellie home on an elephant as it was night-time. They said, "Goodbye,"

Innayah Mirza (7)

Whiteheath Infant & Nursery School, Ruislip

Lucas' Zoo Adventure

...at the big zoo. They met a friendly, heavy elephant, it was grey and big.

Ellie and the elf rode on the grey, heavy elephant and the elephant told them how bamboo grows.

Ellie and the elf went to see the pandas.

Ellie got to feel the mum panda's fur while the elf got to cuddle the little panda but she didn't like it.

Ellie and the elf hopped back onto the tour guide (the elephant) to see the monkeys and apes.

The apes and monkeys liked Ellie so they sat together eating bananas.

It was time for Ellie to go home. The elf and the elephant dropped her off at her house and said goodbye.

Lucas Liu (7)

Whiteheath Infant & Nursery School, Ruislip

Sara's Jungle Adventure

Ellie, Robin and Bear swung on the green, swinging vines in the dark, muddy jungle. After swinging on the long, green vines they went to a green, huge leaf. When they saw the snake behind the leaf they ran away. They ran away as fast as they could. They were so scared. The snake could not catch up with them.

Next, they met a huge lion. They thought the huge lion was scary but really he was nice.

The lion took them on his back. His back was so fluffy. The lion went back to where they started.

The lion let them down to the floor. Ellie and Robin went back home and swung on the vines.

Sara Paloja (7)

Whiteheath Infant & Nursery School, Ruislip

Amir-Saam's Zoo Adventure

...at the zoo. At the door, they met the elephant and they asked him, "Can you show us around please?"
Ellie, her teddy and Robin rode the elephant and Ellie's teddy sat on the trunk. They had lots of fun!
They then spotted the panda and her cub sitting next to the bamboo. The cub was so cute!
Guess where the elephant took them next?
"Look, there's a monkey!"
Ellie and the friendly monkey shared bananas, and they tasted brilliant!
After meeting all the animals and having an amazing adventure, Robin and the elephant took Ellie back home.

Amir-Saam Yazdizad (7)
Whiteheath Infant & Nursery School, Ruislip

Jack's Jungle Adventure

Suddenly they ended up in the jungle. They were swinging on the jungle vines.

"Argh! A snake! Run, run! Fly Elf fly!" But Elf didn't fly, he ran.

"Keep on running until we lose the snake. We are going to lose the snake soon."

"Look!" said Ellie. "There's a lion, let's ride it so we can get away from the snake."

The lion helped Ellie, Elf and Teddy to get nearer to the jungle vines.

Finally, they made it to the vines. Tree to tree they swung back home and had breakfast.

Jack Hine (7)

Whiteheath Infant & Nursery School, Ruislip

Ruby's Zoo Adventure

Ellie and Robin were at the zoo. Ellie was still very tired but she couldn't miss out on all of the fun. In the corner of her eye, she saw an elephant and Ellie, Teddy and Robin rode on the elephant and he took them to every animal in the zoo.

First, they looked at the fluffy, black and white panda.

Next, they went to see the humongous greedy elephant.

They saw a black, silly monkey eating a banana, Ellie had one too.

Robin, Ellie and Teddy rode on the elephant back to Ellie's home. Ellie said bye to Robin.

Ruby Patel (7)

Whiteheath Infant & Nursery School, Ruislip

Manrai's Zoo Adventure

...at the zoo. They saw a yellow and brown giraffe peeking over their fence and a big grey elephant peeking around the door. The elephant said, "Hello."

The elephant said, "Come with me to have a trip to the woods."

First, they went to see the pandas and they even got to hold a baby panda.

Then they had another ride to see something else. Ellie was very excited.

After, they went to see a chimpanzee and they ate some bananas.

Then Robin the elf dropped Ellie at her house and said goodbye.

Manrai Sokhi (7)

Whiteheath Infant & Nursery School, Ruislip

Eliana's Zoo Adventure

Ellie and Robin went to the zoo and they were excited and looking forward to it.

First, they went to see elephants and even rode one. They were high in the sky, they were having fun.

Next, they went to see the pandas and Robin held a baby panda. The pandas were fluffy.

Next, they went onto another elephant and had so much fun.

Next, they went to see the gorillas. The gorillas were eating yellow bananas. Ellie ate a banana as well.

Finally, Ellie was back home and said goodbye to Robin and went back to bed.

Eliana Goodridge (6)

Whiteheath Infant & Nursery School, Ruislip

Esmé's Zoo Adventure

One day Ellie and Robin went to the zoo and they saw a big grey elephant, it was a friendly elephant called Sunny. They climbed onto the elephant with a koala.

Then they saw a panda with its baby and Robin found another panda and held it.

They all went and the elephant took both the koalas on its trunk, while the pandas stayed on the ground.

They saw a monkey eating a banana who put both koalas on the vines.

Robin stayed with the elephant while the koalas stood with Ellie.

They were all so happy.

Esmé Mistry (7)
Whiteheath Infant & Nursery School, Ruislip

Kutay's Jungle Adventure

...a misty, cold jungle. It was scary and ice-cold but it was not going to stop them.

They met a big green snake. They hoped it would not bite, it was yellow and green.

The snake was about to bite but they ran away just in time.

They met a big, fierce lion, it looked friendly. They wondered if they could ride it.

And they could. They shouted, "Yay!" The whole forest could hear them.

Then Robin the elf looked at the sky and told Ellie it was time for bed so they rushed home.

Kutay Baskurt (7)

Whiteheath Infant & Nursery School, Ruislip

Kaiyn's Jungle Adventure

They were swinging over the biggest trees in the multiverse. "Weeeeee!"
Then they fell to the ground and they saw a giant snake and they didn't know what to do.
They were worried so they ran as fast as they could.
They came across a friendly lion in the big bushes and thought they could ask for help.
He said yes! Then soon their adventure through the jungle began!
Soon they reached their swinging branches and they swung all the way back home happily ever after.

Kaiyn Shah (7)
Whiteheath Infant & Nursery School, Ruislip

Connie's Jungle Adventure

Ellie and Robin found themselves in the damp, hot jungle. They swung on thick vines.

They were face-to-face with a snake. The snake went *hissss!* Ellie was frightened.

They zoomed off as the snake rose up like a monster.

Ellie, Teddy and Robin met a lion. The lion said, "Hop on my back."

They did hop on the lion's back!

The lion ran so fast Ellie felt the wind in her hair.

Ellie, Teddy and Robin swung on vines to get home.

Connie Simmons (7)

Whiteheath Infant & Nursery School, Ruislip

Eva's Jungle Adventure

Suddenly Ellie was holding some vines. They swung from one vine to another.

They crashed into a snake. Ellie got scared so she ran away from the snake.

They ran and ran until finally they couldn't see the snake.

They crashed into a lion. Ellie got a bit scared but she didn't run away.

The lion asked if they wanted a ride to the end of the forest.

They swung home on the vines and Robin flew Ellie in through the window and she got in her bed.

Eva Donlevy (7)

Whiteheath Infant & Nursery School, Ruislip

Romeo's Jungle Adventure

...at the jungle. They saw the tall trees and could barely see the sky. Ellie said to Robin, "When I've finished the adventure can I go home?"

Robin and Ellie saw a stripy, big snake. Robin said to Ellie, "This is a scary snake, let's go!"

Ellie and Robin were getting chased by the big scaly snake.

Ellie and Robin saw a big daddy lion.

Robin and Ellie were having a ride on the daddy lion.

Robin and Ellie went back home.

Romeo Hebaj (7)
Whiteheath Infant & Nursery School, Ruislip

Alfie's Zoo Adventure

Ellie suddenly found herself in a zoo. She saw a great, gargantuan elephant.

The elephant took them for a ride to the panda in the enclosure.

They had a look at the stripy black and white panda for a little while.

They took off. They took a ride on the elephant again. They had fun.

They had made it to their destination, the monkeys. They got a banana and strolled back to the elephant.

They stopped at Ellie's house.

Alfie Cooper (7)

Whiteheath Infant & Nursery School, Ruislip

Taileigh's Jungle Adventure

Ellie, Robin and Teddy excitedly enjoyed swinging on the dark green vines.
Suddenly they found themselves in an overgrown colourful jungle.
They accidentally woke up a black and yellow snake. "Run!" they said.
They saw a bright orange, friendly lion.
Teddy, Robin and Ellie got a ride out of the green jungle.
They swung back on the long vines all the way home.

Taileigh Wells (7)

Whiteheath Infant & Nursery School, Ruislip

Blake's Zoo Adventure

...at the zoo. They saw an elephant and rode on it.

Next, they saw some pandas and got to cuddle a mummy panda and her cub.

They got back on the elephant and headed to the next enclosure.

The monkey shared his banana with the little girl.

The elephant took her home.

Blake Phillips-Cavill (7)

Whiteheath Infant & Nursery School, Ruislip

Delylah's Zoo Adventure

...at the zoo. They saw an elephant at the zoo.

They rode the elephant.

The panda was black and white. He was a soft panda.

They rode on the elephant again.

They were eating bananas.

They said goodbye and went home.

Delylah Swift (7)

Whiteheath Infant & Nursery School, Ruislip

Abdullah's Zoo Adventure

Soon they reached the zoo.
They saw an elephant and they rode on it.
They met the panda and hugged him.
They rode on the wrinkly elephant.
They ate bananas...
But it was only a dream.

Abdullah Bhatti (7)

Whiteheath Infant & Nursery School, Ruislip

The Storyboards

Here are the fun storyboards
children could choose from...

MAGICAL ADVENTURE

Jungle Tale

PIRATE ADVENTURE

SPACE STORY

ZOO ADVENTURE

Young Writers Information

We hope you have enjoyed reading this book and that you will continue to in the coming years.

If you're a young writer who enjoys reading and creative writing, or the parent of an enthusiastic poet or story writer, do visit our website **www.youngwriters.co.uk**. Here you will find free competitions, workshops and games, as well as recommended reads, a poetry glossary and our blog.

If you would like to order further copies of this book, or any of our other titles give us a call or visit **www.youngwriters.co.uk**.

Young Writers
Remus House
Coltsfoot Drive
Peterborough
PE2 9BF

(01733) 890066
info@youngwriters.co.uk

Scan to watch the
My First Story video!

YoungWritersUK   YoungWritersCW
youngwriterscw   youngwriterscw